E. Symone Presents

DECEIT

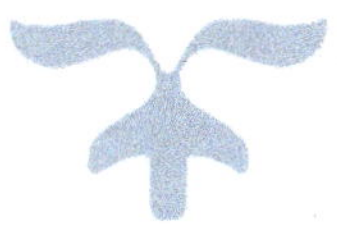

Table Of Contents

Introduction

He teased and kissed my soul on fire

What he left was unsatisfied desire

He left and said he would call soon

But the moon was full

And as we all know

Full moons betray lovers

He did call but only once

To say goodbye

My eyes teared

My gut wrenched

His thirst was quenched

But left me thirsty

He came to me in ecstasy

and I believed he had come for me

– "Deceitful Ecstasy"
by Norberto Franco Cisneros

Chapter 1

The Beginning of the End

As I wipe Lamont's semen mixed with my blood from my inner thighs, I think to myself this will be the last time. The aroma of his malt-liquor body scent on my skin makes my stomach turn. I can't wait to leave this hell hole of a house.

"Chanel, what is takin' yo' ass so long in that bathroom? I'm tired of yo' ass always being in that bathroom using all my shit. Who do you think you are, the queen or something?" my mother yells in a saliva-filled slurred tone from the dingy, broken-down, covered-in-cigarette-burns brown couch that almost touches the floor in the living room. I'm so tired of her, I can't wait until I'm old enough to move out. For one, all she do is sit in the house, smoke her Newports, and turn tricks from time to time. Well, that's when Lamont isn't around, which is when Lamont goes to Inglewood to check on his "ex-wife" and kids. Lamont is a tall, slender man with long, grown-out dreadlocks and dingy brown skin. I would say he usually looks like he drinks a lot and doesn't keep up with himself, but when he goes on his so-called family visits, he is well kept and clean, and he even throws his dreads in a back ponytail instead of all over his face like they are when he is over here. He hasn't shown any divorce papers yet—I am well aware that my mother is his dumbass side chick. What a role model she is.

So, I hurry and rinse the horrible concoction out of the towel and throw it in the hamper so I can see what she wants. Before I even reach the living room, she is already starting her rant on how Lamont messed up her sheets and how I need to hurry up and wash them before one of her clients comes and before her man get back from his kid visit. I roll my eyes. Yeah, right. I honestly don't see how Lamont has the energy to have sex with her, and then right when he is finished, come in my room and take advantage of me. She must not be doing her job right. But I'm going to do what she told me to do, as if I ever have a choice. Getting the house together for my mama to do her job and cleaning up behind her and her man is basically a part of my chores, to keep it simple.

To avoid any confrontation with my mama, it is best to just hurry and get the task done. I stand in her room and contemplate the fastest and easiest way to clean it up in enough time to eat dinner. Sometimes, this two-bedroom house gets so filthy, by the time I am done cleaning up, I am too tired to cook dinner. By that time, dinner usually consists of a pack of chicken ramen noodles and a glass of tap water, if we even have that. My mama doesn't really cook, so it falls back on me. Her dinner is usually a forty ounce of Old English malt liquor and a cigarette. The only time I see her cook, which isn't often and not good, is when Lamont threatens to go back to his ex-wife. But anyway, I continue to get a hot damp towel with Fabuloso on it to scrub her cigarette ashes and semi-fresh semen stains out of her beige sheets. Did you know these are the hardest stains to get out of some sheets? It should be dry before she gets back in the bed. I spray her sheets, comforter, and dingy, formerly white pillows down with Febreze so the bed can be nice and fresh for her drunk ass. Now for the rest of the room, I will leave that for another day because I need to get prepared for tomorrow. I kick her and whoever's clothes under her bed and vacuum the floor. Even the vacuum can't get all of these cigarette ashes and liquor stains out of the dark brown carpet. By the time I'm finished, I'm too tired to cook a full meal for myself, so a Hot Pocket and apple juice is the gourmet dinner for tonight.

Tomorrow is the sophomore pep rally, and my girls and I will be the prettiest ones that Calla View High has ever seen. I have been on DHgate and AliExpress a lot lately, ordering numerous products under different names and saying I did not receive the items to get money. And with all of the products that I receive, I boost them for the low—well, what the people consider low. Who still steals from stores anymore? More risk that isn't worth it. What are we, in the '90s? Anyway, that's how I make my money, and it has been paying off a lot. I have been doing it more than usual so I can afford the things I want so I can look presentable for tomorrow. Yeah, I know, I have no business technically scamming, but what other choice do I have? I have to make money some way, because my mama damn sure doesn't care, and selling ass like her just isn't an option.

Chapter 2

What's Good?

The loud iPhone alarm startles me, blaring in my ear from the side of my bed. I scramble to cut the sound off. Today, it went off at 6:30 a.m. I usually wake up at 7 a.m., but today is special, not really because of the pep rally but because I have been hearing that my crush, Devion, plans on approaching me with something special to say today. This honestly surprised me to hear because we have never talked, only glanced at one another in the hallway from time to time, with him being a senior and all. That's normal at our school, for sophomores and seniors not to really talk. But if he comes up and says hi, that's fine with me.

So, I jump in the shower, brush my teeth, comb my body wave bundles, do my eyebrows, and glue my mink lashes on. I don't use too much makeup because I really don't need it. With my beautiful deep-chestnut skin tone and tall, slim-but-thick figure, I don't need too many enhancements. Beauty like this does come at a price for a fifteen-year-old like myself, though— attention from child predators like Lamont, for example. Anyway, today, I'm just going to wear a fitted beige jumpsuit from Fashion Nova that hugs my small hips and shows what little breast that I do have. I top it off with my gold hoops and rhinestone sandals. Something simple but cute.

While I'm headed toward the front door, I hear Mama and Lamont fighting about something in the kitchen, which is nothing new; they fight at least once a day. Mama will get tired of it eventually. Before I can even make it to the door, I hear tussling as if they're shoving one another, but that's none of my business. The best thing I can do for her in these situations is pray for her and keep it pushing. It's not like she is going to ever leave him alone. I roll my eyes and walk out, letting the screen door slam behind me.

I arrive at school in enough time to get some breakfast and meet up with my girls Merceedes and Lynn. They haven't arrived yet; I'm usually the first one here because I live the closest to school, about a fifteen-minute walk from my house to here. As I sit down in the cafeteria and scroll on Instagram to try to look busy since no one I hang with has arrived yet, I hear someone from behind me say in a low, seductive voice, "I see you tryna look good for Daddy."

I jump and turn around, but before I can say, "What the—" I realize it's Merceedes's childish ass holding back animated laughter. One thing about Merceedes, she loves to play and joke, but she has the worst temper. Sometimes, I call her Tas for short because when she is mad, she turns into the Tasmanian devil. I've noticed some of the prettiest girls have the worst attitudes, and Merceedes has a beautiful mahogany skin tone with long, kinky-curly natural hair with an over-developed coke-bottle shape. All of the boys, from freshmen to seniors at our school, lust for her. Sometimes, I even get a little jealous, but we have been best friends since the third grade, and I don't see that changing any time soon.

I can't help but laugh with Merceedes at how she scared me like that, but I don't know why she is playing. She knows I'm already on pins and needles over the rumor about Devion approaching me today.

"Girl, stop playing! How do I look? You think Devion is really going to come up to me today?!" I ask anxiously while we sit down across from one another.

Merceedes rolls her eyes and says, "Of course. Why wouldn't he? How you're looking today, he is going to say something regardless."

Before I can even respond, Lynn finally walks up with her preppy ass. "Hey, ladies, we are going to have an eventful day today!" Lynn is such a sweetheart, sometimes I wonder how she can stay positive with everything that she has been through. Lynn just moved to Compton from Calabasas, a major social-class jump, right? Well, her father is—or should I say *was* a big-time investor who got caught up in some white-collar crime shit, which led to him getting incarcerated, which resulted in Lynn, her mother, and her brother downsizing to more affordable housing in the hood. I would describe Lynn as a sweet brunette white girl that can be naïve at times. Although she can be naïve, her heart is genuine, which is one of the reasons why I took her under my wing fast. I mostly hang with her during school hours, though, because in her spare time, she likes to kick back and go do coke with her old friends, and I ain't into all of that.

"Before I forget to tell y'all, before we enter the pep rally, let's all meet at the bathroom by the cafeteria so we can all walk in together," I tell the girls.

They responded in unison, "We went over this numerous times!"

I'm just trying to let them know because I'll be damned if I am standing by myself when Devion walks up to me. The bell rings, and we do our group handshake and go our separate ways for the morning. As I'm walking to class, I feel this slight tap on my shoulder. I hope this isn't Merceedes's ass playing again.

As I turn around, my breath is taken by this handsome boy with a dark Hershey complexion, hazel eyes, thick, luscious eyebrows, deep black waves from the pacific in his hair, and a tall, muscular physique. He kind of looks like one of them niggas from a *Jet* magazine or something. As I am trying to play cool and observe how attractive he is, I am interrupted by him saying, "What up, doe? My name is Devion, and I have been seeing you around. You kinda cute. You should fuck with me sometimes." He looks down at me with a small, charming smirk.

"Well, my name is Chanel, if you wanted to know, and . . . umm, I'll think about it. You don't sound like you from around here." I have to play it cool. I mean, he cute, don't get me wrong, but I'm not about to be out here looking desperate. Hell, he gotta work for this. I don't know why I'm playing—if he say and do the right things, I'm going to bust it open like a can of pringles. I can see us getting married now.

I snap out of my daydream as he proceeds to tell me he is from Detroit. Sounds like a plus to me, something different from what I am used to seeing. He continues, "You will think about it? Ha! But enough of me, wassup with you? You got a number? Or Instagram?"

I hand him my phone in slow motion. We exchange numbers and Instagram names, and I am so wrapped up in what we have going on, I almost forget I am on my way to class. Needless to say, our conversation is cut short and we head our separate ways. I'm feeling him already, but we are going to see what's good. Before he reaches the end of the hallway to turn, he tells me he's going to see me at the pep rally. Me being me, have to keep it cool, I say, "Yeah, okay, see you around." Then I fast-walk to the classroom so he won't see the Kool-Aid smile spreading across my face.

Chapter 3

Good Form

All of the students are bombarding their way into the large gymnasium. It's so packed, I can barely find the meeting spot that my girls and I agreed to meet one another at. I almost miss it, until I see Merceedes and Lynn waving their hands at me by the entrance. I jog my way over to them, trying to hurry up so I can tell them this hot tea on what happened earlier. But there are too many people swarming the area, so we focus on finding a good seat in the bleachers for the pep rally instead.

As we sit down, I can't keep it to myself anymore. I am bursting with excitement. "Y'all, Devion got my nnuummbberr!"

Lynn laughs and stomps her foot. "What I tell you!"

While we laugh, rocking back and forth with our hands over our mouths, I notice Merceedes isn't as interested as I expected. Lynn proceeded to ask Merceedes, "What is wrong with you? You're missing all of the tea."

Merceedes responds in irritation, "I heard y'all, but my mama is texting me tripping." She proceeds to put her phone into her back pocket and talk about a party she wants us to attend with her this weekend. We brush it off and continue to enjoy the pep rally.

Our principal comes out and amps up the crowd while the varsity basketball players run out, and down comes Devion, looking so irresistible. "There goes my man!" I yell in Lynn's ear, laughing.

"They really are such a hype, honestly, they cool but not that good. Y'all need to chill," Merceedes says in a playful tone.

Personally, I just care about one person on the team, and we all know who that is. Basketball isn't really my sport, so Merceedes's comment doesn't get to me. I notice Lynn starting to get a little irritated with the vibes that Merceedes is giving off, but I'm feeling like, *fuck it!* It's Friday, my crush approached me, it can't get no better than this. Whatever ruined Merceedes's day is going to have to wait for another day.

After the pep rally, school is over. I thought we were going to hang out for a little after school, but Lynn says her mom is in the front of the school waiting for her. So, I guess we won't be hanging with her. Merceedes and I decide not to hang around the school. She walks with me toward home, since we stay a couple of blocks by each other.

I'm bursting with enthusiasm, telling her every detail on what just happened, and she is responding with little comments like, "Oh, yeah," and, "Wow," but she still seems preoccupied on her phone. I know I don't need all of her attention, but that's what she usually gives, and I'm telling her some real interesting shit, so she needs to fully listen. Then again, maybe I am being self-absorbed, so I switch up the conversation and ask her what is going on.

Merceedes responds with a slight smile. "Girl, nothing, just arguing with these niggas, you know they can't get enough of me. I be having to tell them to chill sometimes." She continues looking down at her phone.

By this time, we are getting close to my block, since I don't live far from the school. I want to bring Devion up one more time since it looks like Merceedes is coming back around. "Girl, what do you think about what happened today?!" I say, smiling and nudging Merceedes's arm.

She says I need to chill and act like I am used to talking to boys, but the next moment, someone calls her and she speed-walks away from me to the other side of the street, going past my block and saying she will catch up with me later today. I brush it off and continue home.

Hopefully, Devion hits me up today. That would make my day even better. Not that I am thirsty or anything.

Chapter 4

Nothing but a Number

"First off, she is a young little broad. I don't see why you're even looking her way when you got a whole baby on the way," Marcus tells me as he passes the blunt in the smoky, hotboxed '09 Impala.

I lock my phone from showing him Chanel's Instagram picture. "One, she is not that young, and I don't even know if the fucking baby is mines. Plus, ol' girl seems different. I'ma see what the vibe is."

Marcus is a fucking hater. I really think he low-key mad he didn't get on ol' girl before me. I only keep his ass around because he is more loyal than a lot of these niggas. But even that is neither here nor there; he can switch up anytime. One thing I learned about friends, keep them at arm's length.

"Alright, nigga, I'ma have to get home before my mama start tripping," I say as I buckle my seatbelt and sit up, ready to go. Really a subtle way to tell Marcus to get the fuck out without saying or doing much.

We finish our smoke session and I drop Marcus off at home. He was starting to get on my nerves, and I gotta hurry home so I can avoid my mama's mouth. It's getting pretty late anyway. Damn! I almost forgot today is my Mama's birthday, we should be expecting some family to come by and kick it for a little bit. I would invite Chanel, but nahh, it's too early for that. And I don't want them to bring up this baby situation, either. My mama don't know how to hold her water for shit.

She been told numerous times not to say nothing until after the DNA test is done. I mean, yeah, I slept with the bitch, but she is for everybody. Last I heard, she was fucking with one of my patnas from Slauson.

As I pull up to the house, I notice the block is already cracking, cars parked on both sides of the street up and down my block. Even though my mama and I are from Detroit, most of her daddy's side is from Cali, so that's what brought us out this way some years ago. I park my car a block over and proceed in the house. Right when I open the screen door, the smells of marijuana, alcohol, and party wings caress my nose.

"Aye, nephew, come get yo' ass kicked at this spade table real quick!" one of my three uncles yells from the round table in the back of the kitchen. I love them niggas. With my daddy being in and out of my life, they have been the only men that stuck. They taught me about life, women, and even money. They are really making me who I am today, along with my mama, of course.

I make my way to the back of the house, where the kitchen is, to show these old niggas wassup. Before I can even sit down comfortably, here they go with the questions.

"I heard you have a baby on the way, who is it by? You don't believe in condoms? You moving too stupid in these streets. I thought I told you to let them suck it, not stick it." They all was asking questions and saying comments in rotation. They all always have an opinion about something. I get the whole tough-love concept, but sometimes it gets very annoying. I know for a fact, each of my uncles has made a female get an abortion before. I would know because my mama told me, but I'ma let them have it.

"While y'all are worried about me, y'all need to be worried about this spade game. I got it handled. I ain't even worried about all of that." We all laugh and continue the game, but my Uncle Smoke can't seem to let it go. He has to come at me on some philosophy shit.

"You know I love you, so I'ma just keep it real with you. Having a child is a big responsibility, so however this ends, be a man and take care of your business."

All of my uncles continue to nod their heads, and I understand. Out of all of my uncles, Peanut, Mace, and Smoke, Smoke is my favorite. Even though they all help raise me, he has been around the most. Hell, before he got married and found God, he even stayed with us for a little. Even though I don't like to hear certain advice, I take what he says to heart. He been through a lot of shit, which makes me look up to him more. I know he won't steer me in the wrong direction.

"I got this, like I said, we good," I respond with agitation. What he said is really resonating in my mind.

I make up an excuse to leave the table because I know they aren't just going to stop there. "But alright, y'all, as much as I would like to whoop y'all in spades, let me go talk to my mama before it becomes my funeral along with her birthday," I say as I get up from the table. My uncles laugh and smirk. They already know what I am on and not trying to hear. I grab a chicken wing by the stove and make my way to the living room. I am greeted by my mother's contagious laugh, and before I can take another bite of my wing, she grabs my hand, initiating a classic two-step to some old-school Earth, Wind & Fire. She has wine in one hand and my hand in the other, and I can't help but laugh and dance with her while her friends and family cheer us on in the middle of the living room. Earth, Wind & Fire has some long-ass songs, but it finally finishes, and we laugh and make our way to the finely decorated blue-and-silver couch.

"Happy birthday, Mama." I give her a kiss on her forehead. Then, though I don't want to ruin the moment, I can't help myself. "Why did you tell the family I have a baby on the way? You know I don't like people in my business."

Mama frowned up and scooted away, saying in an irritated tone, "It's my birthday, which means I don't care about none of your irresponsible bullshit you have going on. And yes, I told them, because let's not act like you didn't have the girl over here every weekend and after school. So I'm not even surprised you're in the boat you're in, and why did they tell you that? I told them not say nothin'."

I just get up and walk away, upstairs to my room. It's funny how women can twist shit on you and make you look wrong. I know it's a possibility I could be wrong, and I was busting her down without a rubber, but shit, other niggas get away with it. How could I know she would get pregnant? Shouldn't she be on birth control, anyway?

But shit, let me get my mind off this and hit up Chanel before it's too late. I can't let that slip between my fingers.

Chapter 5

What the Business Is?!

I knew it was too good to be true. Devion still hasn't hit me up yet, and it's damn near 10 p.m., but whatever, it's all good. At least I can sit back and enjoy my own company tonight. Since it's Friday, Mama will be "working" on Skid Row, so I know she won't be in until tomorrow morning. And the argument Mama had with Lamont earlier must have been a little serious because he's usually home when I get out of school, but it wasn't like that today. Hopefully, he stays gone. Tonight will be a typical night for me; scrolling on Instagram and watching some Netflix is how I spend my nights. Usually, I would go to Merceedes's house on the weekends to escape from here, but her mama must be trippin' or something because I haven't been invited over there these past three weekends, which is kinda funny because what else could Merceedes be doing instead of trying to hang with me? And our walk home was kind of awkward. We didn't laugh or talk much, so she must've really had something going on today. I will catch up with her later.

Whatever, let me cut this music on and vibe. As I turn on "Hrs & Hrs" by Muni Long, my mother interrupts my Friday-night vibe. By throwing open my door and saying, "You ain't grown listening to this type of music, but how do I look?" She does a slow spin in her leopard-print dress that hugs her, what I refer to as, "mom bod." My mama is a very beautiful woman. She has a slim figure, which is probably where I get it from.

Although she is pretty skinny, her butt and breasts are bigger than mine, her breasts just aren't as perky as mine. She has a beautiful, smooth caramel complexion that sparkles in the sun and pretty, straight teeth. I would say white, but with all of the cigarettes she smokes, her teeth have a brown tint to them. She keeps her hair in a short, curly pixie cut. If I could compare her to someone, I would say she resembles Nia Long from *Friday*, just an older version. She is so intelligent, at least when she is not drunk, which is very seldom. At times, I don't understand why my mama chose this profession of prostitution and puts up with these different men. One day, she did slip up and tell me she had thought she had a future with my father because he comes from money, but after I was born, he was gone with the wind. Typical no-good men shit.

"Yes, Mama, you look fine. What time will you be in, anyway?" Before she can respond, I notice I got an incoming FaceTime call. Oh, shit! It's Devion. "Mama, get out! I got an important call coming in!"

I shove her out of my room and make sure my hair is still laid to prepare for this first call. Before answering the phone, I look in my dresser mirror in front of my bed to make sure my appearance is giving what it is supposed to give, then run myself through a little pep talk, like, *I mean, it's me, the one and only Chanel. Like, c'mon now! Of course, he is going to want to call me!*

"Wassup?" I say in a sweet but cool tone, holding the phone at an angle so he doesn't see too much but enough of my background and face. When I say Devion is looking good, he is looking GOODT on this FaceTime call.

He smiles and says, "'Sup, baby, wassup with you? What you on tonight?"

"Nothing really, might hit up a party tonight. Usually, every other Friday, I'm at somebody's party." Me lying through my teeth trying to sound interesting.

"Oh, okay. Well, hit my line when you leave the party, then."

"I mean, well, I probably won't even go. I ain't really feeling it tonight." Trying to cover up my lie. I hope his ass didn't notice. Now, I am ready to hang up.

"Look at you. Stop playing, girl, and let's chill. I ain't gon' bite." We both burst out in laughter. He's smarter than what I thought.

"Why do you want to pull up so bad? I hope you don't think I am one of these easy girls running around here. We just met," I tell him with attitude.

"Chiilll, you think I'm one of them, Chanel? I'm really just tryna chill, that's all."

I went ahead and gave him my address. We are going to hang out, two hours max! I don't need him going back to school on Monday saying it only took him one day to hit because I'm technically still a virgin, anyway. I have not willingly had sex with anyone, a couple of make-out sessions with some boys here and there, but that's how far things ever went. If I am going to give it up to anyone, they are definitely going to have to be worth it.

Forty-five minutes has barely passed, and I already have an incoming text from Devion saying he is outside. Luckily, my mama already left to work some minutes ago—the last thing I need is to be embarrassed by my mama. Let me just take my time heading out to his car because I'm not trying to come off as too excited and thirsty. I'm going to just slip on some fitted black leggings and a black-and-pink crop-top hoodie that shows my belly-button piercing. I mean, let's face it, giving him a little eye candy won't hurt.

As I make my way to the front door, I double-check to make sure that my mama is already gone to work. I don't wanna be answering any questions. As I ease into the car, I am slapped with the luring smell of Black Ice and Ralph Lauren Polo Blue cologne. To set the relaxing tone, Devion has some smooth '90s R&B playing, which eases a little of the tension. We continue to make small talk, but I can tell he really has more things on his mind than just pulling up to talk about basic shit. We could have done this over the phone.

"You smoke? I just want to check before I roll up."

"Clearly, I'm a whole stoner out here. You better not have some bullshit," I say with a smirk. Here I go, lying once again. I really don't smoke.

Devion rolls up the weed, and we start to smoke. The soft smoke fills my lungs and makes my body relax so much, it kind of startles me. I'm not sure if it's him or the weed, but I've become very comfortable and giggly. We begin to talk about everything pertaining to life, ambitions, and even relationships. I find him even more attractive now I know there is more to him than his good looks. I'm enjoying his company so much that these two hours have felt like two minutes.

"Damn, time went by fast! It's almost three something," I say, trying to think of ways to get in the house before my mama comes home.

Devion looks at his phone. "Yeah, it's getting pretty late. Let me make it home before my mama notices I'm gone."

Right before I hop out the car, we lock eyes, gazing longingly at one another, which makes my heart race and panties wet off of the vibe we're giving each other. Right before our lips touch, I look away and stumble out the car. "See you later," I say nervously. I can't believe we almost kissed. He must really like me . . . we did have a vibe going. All of these thoughts are racing through my head as I walk in the house. I wonder what's next?!

When I get to my door, I look over my shoulder to see if he's pulled off yet. To my surprise, he's still sitting there with the window rolled down, watching me get in the house. I am even more impressed; any other boy would have driven off, especially if they didn't get none. I hurry up and go in the house, and right when I close the door, I press my back against it and slide down, laughing hysterically. No boy has ever made me feel like this. I can't wait to tell the girls what happened.

I finally get washed up and settle into bed. Lynn didn't answer my FaceTime call, and neither did Merceedes. Oh, well, I will try to call them again sometime tomorrow or just update them on Monday.

Chapter 6

What About Your Friends

Couple of weeks have passed since my car session with Devion, and we have been hitting it off pretty hard. During these past weeks, we have been talking on the phone more, he has been walking me to classes, and he even introduced me to some of his close friends, but we still haven't kissed or done anything yet. I find him very patient—he doesn't try to push up on me, and we don't even talk about sex. I love that we are establishing a bond without it being based around sex. But I will say, every time we are around each other, it does cross my mind.

Life is really amazing right now. Lamont hasn't been around at all lately, so I guess their last argument was something serious, or his wife took his ass back. Either way, he hasn't been around me, and that's all I care about. The house has been peaceful since he left. Mama is still passed out every day, nothing new, and the little time that she is sober, I have noticed her constantly calling Lamont, cursing him out. Like, move on and do better, gahdamn!

Devion wants to ride and get ice cream this evening, so to avoid him possibly encountering my drunk mama, I may just go by Merceedes's house so he can just pick me up there. The last thing I want is him to see my mama in one of her drunk rages or her passed out naked in a random place of the house. But Merceedes has been on some bullshit lately, not really answering the phone, and she hasn't been talking to me much at school. The times we have talked, it has seemed uneasy. I get the feeling she is low-key jealous because I haven't done anything to her ass. Lynn even noticed her shift in attitude. We barely see her around school, and she doesn't walk home with me anymore. Fuck it, she only stays three blocks away from me, anyway. I'm going to walk over there real quick and get this settled.

The walk to Merceedes's house is not the problem, it's the damn crackheads, drunks, and undercover pimps on the street that are the problem. As I stroll through the streets of Compton, I enjoy the urban scenery while the song "Everybody Loves the Sunshine" by Roy Ayers Ubiquity fill my ears with its beautiful melody, loud through my AirPods. I know these streets can be cruel, but something about California will always have a hold on me, no matter how raunchy and heartless these streets can be.

Let me put some pep in my step because 6 p.m. will be here in no time for Devion to pull up, and he do be on time. I arrive to Merceedes's house, and I notice her mama is home because her smooth silver 2020 Lexus sedan is parked in the driveway. Her mother is always so welcoming and well put together. One thing about Merceedes is she comes from a good background, an active father who is a barber and a hairstylist mother who loves and nurtures her. What more could a girl want? Her parents are pretty strict. At first, I didn't understand, but I've come to realize, why wouldn't they be? If I had active parents that cared about me, I would expect the same.

I ring the doorbell, hoping Merceedes will answer the door so we can get this over with and I can lace her up on what has really been going on at home and with Devion. Instead, her timid and awkward older brother answers the door with a shy smile. "Hey, Chanel, I haven't seen you around here lately. I'll go get Merceedes," he says and walks off fast, before I can even see how he has been.

Well, that was odd. Usually, he lets me in, and I go get her myself. Whatever, all of these people are on some other shit today. Merceedes comes to the door with an irritated look on her face. She doesn't even look well put together like she usually does. Her hair is in a messy bun, she has a dingy, loose white T-shirt and loose gray sweatpants on. Sis is looking tore down at this moment. I am shocked by it, honestly, because she normally keeps me on my toes when it comes to appearances. I know she is just at her house, but damn, I must have caught her on her only bad day.

"Wassup?" Merceedes says in irritation as she rolls her neck.

"Hey . . . Well, I haven't hung out with you in a while, so I wanted to stop by to see how you are doing. I haven't even had time to lace you up on what is new with me and Devion."

"Girl, ain't nobody worried about you and that nigga, but I have been busy, so when I have time, I will hit you up. Cool?"

Before I can even decide whether to respond or slap the fuck out of her, she slams her door in my face. Tears sting my eyes as I storm off, trying to fight the temptation to turn around and bust her door down. We have been close for so long, for her to act like this out of the blue, my assumptions might really be true, she is jealous! All of them boys that she talks to, and she don't want to be excited for me and mines? Alright. Maybe I am looking at this wrong, maybe her parents are getting a divorce or something, which is making her hate the world. It would be one thing if I would have done something to her, but I didn't. I'm going to call Lynn while I'm walking back home and see if she knows anything. I don't usually call her after school hours, but I will see . . .

To my surprise, Lynn answers the FaceTime call.

"Girl, why is Merceedes acting funny and slamming the door in my face?!"

"She hasn't been talking much to me either, I was going to ask you same thing because you know her better than I do!" Lynn exclaims.

"Girl, I don't know, she was on one today." While I'm talking, I notice loud pop music and laughter in the background. Lynn laughs and seems preoccupied.

"We will talk about it more on Monday, girl, I'm at this pool party and it's getting loud. Love ya!" Lynn says, rushing me off the phone. I can't expect her to be too concerned; she hasn't been our friend long enough to know how deep this really runs.

As soon as I walk through the door, I get an incoming text message from Devion. "I'm five minutes away, see you soon, baby."

I hurry up and refresh my deodorant and put on something comfortable. By this time, another text has come in saying that he is here.

Our date went well. He took me to this local ice-cream shop in the neighborhood. This day couldn't have been any better, despite the whole Merceedes shit. We pull up to my house, and Devion comes and opens my door. I feel like everything is moving in slow motion, like a movie, when he says, "I have really been hitting it off with you, and I really want to take us serious. Well, that is, if you want to."

The way he is looking in my eyes, it feels like every word he is saying is touching my soul. Being wrapped in his arms, feeling his hands caress my lower back, I am ready to risk it all. I respond in a soft voice, "I wouldn't have it any other way." Our lips softly touch one another as our eyes close in pleasure. I can't help but feel him getting aroused as I push up on him longingly, wanting him to take It to that next level, but I have to stop myself because deep down, I am still skeptical of having sex willingly for the first time.

Chapter 7

Knight in Shining Armor

"Well, did you finally tell her you got a baby on the way? If you are going to get serious with her like you say, then she has the right to know," Marcus's hating ass exclaims.

"You more worried about the baby than I am. I will tell her when all of this is figured out. Until then, I'm only worried about Chanel," I reply in utter frustration, still looking at the television screen as we play 2K in my room. I only called this nigga to chop it up and talk about what could be next for Chanel and myself. I should have known he was going to come up with that. I really should have kept the secret to myself. It has been a lot going on for me this year; senior year is already eventful enough. It's hard balancing these hoes, trying to get a basketball scholarship to one of my dream schools, Duke, and this baby situation. I'm really just trying to prosper and do something with my life and not deal with bullshit commentary from my so-called friends. That nigga need to focus on what he is doing with his life instead of worrying about me.

All of this is becoming overwhelming. I'm shocked myself that I am putting in so much effort for Chanel when it's hoes that will give it up on the first day. Something about her is different, though, and I like it for some reason. Shit, I'm not even worried about sex when it comes to her; our vibe is on a whole different level. What I do need to stop is fucking ol' girl who claims she is having my baby. It's not an everyday thing, but I am still tapping in from time to time. She for the streets, anyway, I know for a fact she with more niggas than me. We probably need to talk about getting her an abortion before I get in too deep with Chanel.

We been playing 2K for some hours, and my phone keeps blowing up. Who is that calling back-to-back? Chanel?! I wonder if she is mad I didn't call when I got home or something. As I answer the phone, she is crying hysterically. "Can you please come pick me up? I can't take this anymore!"

I drop my controller and get up to head straight to her house. "I got you, I'm on my way!"

I wonder what the fuck could be going on . . .

"Marcus, it's some shit I have to handle real quick, I'ma catch up with you later," I tell him while walking out the room.

Marcus follows. "Nigga, you need me to ride with you? What is going on?" he says while trying to keep up with me.

"Nah, I need to handle this alone. I don't even know what is going on." I hop in the car, trying to put it in reverse before I even fully cut it on. I can see Marcus standing in the yard, looking confused and irritated, wondering what just happened, but I don't care. I gotta go.

Chapter 8

This Is It

I hope I didn't send the wrong message to Devion about our first kiss. I left so awkward and fast because I got nervous. I really hope he don't think I didn't enjoy it, but I haven't even heard from him since he left. Well, what a way to end a great day, overall.

As I gather my underwear, bra, and pajamas for my shower, I notice Lamont is back. He left his wallet on the kitchen table, and when he is here, my mama closes her door with the music blasting. Hopefully, he chooses to stay away from me tonight. This shit is really getting old . . . since my mama don't take up for me, I am going to start taking up for myself. I get my hot, steamy shower ready and hop in. This is the perfect time to reflect on all the activities that have taken place within these last weeks. Working on something with my crush, that is going great. Friends-wise, things are shaky, and house-wise, ain't shit changed but the days. With Devion graduating this year, I wonder where that would leave us? Oh, well, let me just enjoy him while he is here. Whatever happens, happens, at this point. I get out the shower, dry off, and get myself together. Hopefully, Devion has texted me by now.

I haven't received anything yet, and it is getting late. I will just call it a night and hit him up in the morning. As I get comfortable in my full-size bed and slowly drift into what I would call a good night's sleep, I feel a coarse hand creep up my shorts and hot breath tingle down my back. I turn around and try to push

Lamont off, but before I can even fully extend my arm, I am pounced on and choked. Lamont's are hands wrapped around my throat like how a boa constrictor strangles its prey, and with all of his weight on my upper torso, I know I have to move fast before I lose consciousness.

"Bitch, you better not fight and take this dick," his dark silhouette says to me in a raspy, slurred voice. Tears start to prick my eyes as I continue to try to break away from his strong grasp and clamp my legs together so his erect dick won't be able to force its way in.

I finally get his grip loose enough to where I can bite his hand to get him at least halfway off of me. I bite his hand to the point where I can taste pure iron at the tip of my tongue. Lamont jumps back and screams with pain but cocks his fist back and punches me right in my nose. As blood gushes from my nose and my vision goes blurry, all I can hear is Lamont screaming, "You dirty hoe! How dare you!"

My mama must have heard all of the commotion because she stumbles in with a stunned look on her face. I thought this would be the one moment where she'd take up for me and this could all end, but she says, "Bitch, are you trying to get with my man?! I knew yo' fast ass been trying to fuck him."

I don't get shocked much, but that just took the cake. "Mama, are you fucking serious?! Your so-called man been taking advantage of me, and you have been ignoring what he has been doing time and time again!" I scream with blood and tears on my face, still trying to catch my breath. While my mama is trying to console Lamont and hold him back, I call the only person who I feel I can depend on at this moment, Devion. I can't even control my emotions when he finally picks up, but I hear him say he is on his way.

"It's fine, Mama, you and your man don't have to worry about me. Fuck you and that nigga! I'm done. I cannot deal with any of this anymore," I say as I try to hurry up and pack as many things as I can in my pink duffel bag and large Juicy Couture suitcase. Before I can finish gathering my things, I feel a strong pull on my ponytail, jerking me back and causing me to get dragged onto the wood-linoleum floor of my room.

My mother continues to drag me on the floor, punching me upside my temple and screaming, "I can't stand hoes like you always trying to push up on my man! Bitch, ain't no running away. You can't come back, period!"

I grab ahold of my ponytail, managing to flip around and out of my mother's grasp. I pounce on top of her and begin to punch her in her face repeatedly, until I am suddenly grabbed and put up against the wall by Devion. Things are so hectic in here, I didn't even notice he had come in, let alone arrived at my house. That was quick.

"What the fuck is going on, Chanel?!" Devion exclaims as he is trying to keep me in the corner to defuse the situation.

I try to explain to him what is going on, but with all of this going on, my words can't come out right, just sobs and words here and there. "My-my-my mama's boyfriend . . . has been raping me for years! And-and I'm the bad guy?!" I say, still trying to catch my breath.

Devion notices Lamont walking toward the doorway, lighting a cigarette. "Uncle Smoke?" he says with a confused look. Devion starts to breathe hard, as if something horrible is arising from within.

Lamont must realize he is in too deep, so might as well say fuck it. A devious grin slowly appears on his face, but before he can take another puff of his cigarette, Devion punches the shit out of his temple. That makes Lamont fall straight to the ground, but even as he's falling, Devion keeps punching him and punching him until his fists are covered with blood. I try to pull Devion off with all of the strength that I have left, and my mama is hitting Devion in the back to get off Lamont. He finally comes to his senses and stops, and he rises up off of Lamont. Lamont just sits there and laughs, covered in blood.

While my mama's busy consoling Lamont, Devion helps gather all of my packed belongings, and then we are on our way out. Before I leave, I turn around in the hallway and tell my mama, "You may not ever feel bad for this, but just know, you are dead to me."

Devion and I walk out the door, and the last I hear from my mama is, "Fuck you, you and that nigga get out of my house!"

Chapter 9

New Woman

I couldn't help but notice the look on Devion's face while he put my stuff in the car, along with still being a gentleman and helping me get in the car. It was so much going on, it's hard to process what just happened. I don't know how to talk to Devion about this, but the conversation needs to take place.

The ride to Devion's house is long and quiet, even though it's the middle of the night. He stays on a better side of Compton. I was on the north; he stays more toward the southwest of Dominguez Hills.

On one hand, I am beyond relieved to finally get away from the years of agony I have encountered, then on the other hand, I am embarrassed we are just now getting interested in each other, and now he knows how dysfunctional my household really is. While we ride to his house, I put the seat back a little and gaze at the dark sky and stars. I'm really done with that house. I don't know what the future has in store for me, but anything is better than the situation I just left.

We pull up in the driveway of his well-kept, upper-middle-class home. Before he says anything, I break the silence. "I don't have anyone, my grandparents stay in the south and don't have any dealings with my mama whatsoever, and my father and his family, I have no idea where they are at, and shit, when it comes to friends . . . I just have no one." Tears begin to roll down my face as I try to explain my life in bits and pieces. I try to continue, but words won't come.

Devion grabs my face passionately and says, "Fuck them, you don't need nobody but me! As long as I'm here, I got you."

"But what about your mother? She doesn't know me, and we just found out your uncle, which is probably her brother, was the one raping me."

"One thing about my mama, she don't play that funny shit, and when she finds out about this, he will have to worry about way more than the fight I had with his ass."

We get out the car and go in the house, and I stand behind Devion because I don't really know what to expect at this point. His mother comes down the stairs, not noticing I am behind him, saying, "Now, why did you run out of my house like that when—" Before she can finish, she notices my beat-up face and his bruised and bloody fists. "Lord, have mercy! What is going on?! What happened? Are y'all okay?! Devion, get to explaining, NOW!" she says as she rushes toward us in urgency and concern.

He tells his mother what all happened and all that her brother and my mother have done to me. By the end of the conversation, her eyes are full of tears. She sits by me with sympathy and pain in her eyes and embraces me with a warm hug. It is the only sense of nurturing I've felt in years, and it feels good. His mama pulls back and looks at me and says, "I want you to know what was done to you was completely wrong, and we don't roll like that over here. Based off of what has happened, I don't even want to claim my brother after this. This isn't the end of that, and I will make sure that you don't return that house."

By the time I get adjusted and comfortable in bed, it is almost two o'clock in the morning. Devion has a well put-together room upstairs, mostly basketball posters and video games everywhere, which I should have known. He showed me where the bathroom was so I could take a shower and wash all of the negativity and scent of that house, period, off of me. I felt so much better after that shower, it seems as if the warm water washed away all of my worries. Everything in this house is so well kept. Everything is clean, smells good, there are clean towels, cold central air. I felt like I was in a nice hotel for a little bit.

As I fluff the pillow and move around to get comfortable in his queen-size bed, I feel him ease into the bed with his white T-shirt and basketball shorts on. He pauses to make sure I am comfortable enough to sleep beside him, but I'm fine with it; I'd rather sleep in his arms tonight.

Devion turns on his fifty-inch flat-screen to ESPN, which does not surprise me. I turn around and lay my head on his chest, listening to his heartbeat as he rubs my back ever so softly. With every stroke of his hand up and down my back, I feel a tingle inside. I am so compelled to put my hands down his boxers and see how far we can go. So, I slowly slide my hands down his boxers and lightly stroke his dick in an up-and-down motion. Before he gives into the pleasure that I am trying to give him, he stops me and whispers, "Are you sure you want to do this?"

I rise up and suck on his bottom lip. Before I know it, he's on top of me, swirling his tongue in between my lower lips, causing me to release sounds of pleasure. He begins to get harder and harder from the actions taking place in what once was his simple teenage abode. I feel myself become more wet against his warm mouth as the passion in his touch and actions becomes more intense. He slides me slowly toward the edge of the bed, putting my legs on his shoulders and hovering over me, to the point where my feet are behind my head. He slides his long, hard shaft inside of me, causing me to become louder with the noises I continue to make. To stop his mother from coming in and interrupting a never-ending love session, he begins to kiss me, and I let out my love tunes inside of his mouth until we both orgasm in unison, wrapped up in one another. After we come down from the long overdue encounter, Devion holds me from the back, and we fall asleep in each other's juices until the following day.

That morning, I wake up feeling like a new and improved woman. Every time I think about officially being out of Mama's household, I rejoice with happiness. Zoning out of my thoughts, I turn around to be greeted by Devion, to notice he is already out of the bed. Why would he leave me in this room by myself, knowing I don't know this house or his mama like that? I leave the room and follow the smells of pancakes, sizzling sausage, and eggs. I'm not used to this, a mother up this early in the morning, let alone cooking. I make my way into the kitchen to find his mama is cooking, dancing to Frankie Beverly and Maze. Based off of my observations, she is more on the old-school side. She is a heavy-set woman with a beautiful smile, and she gives off a calm, nurturing vibe. I can get used to this, if she allows it.

She didn't notice me standing in the doorway admiring her dance moves and cooking at first, and it startles her when she does. She grabs her chest and chuckles, waving me in to sit down at the round table in the corner of the kitchen. As I sit down, she tells me, "I wasn't able to introduce myself last night. My name is Cheryl, but you can call me Mama C. Now, on Sundays in this house, we go to church, but since you are getting adjusted, we won't go this weekend. Do you go to church?"

I shake my head and look down at the table bashfully. "All of this is kind of new to me. My mama never took me to church."

"Well, there is a first time for everything, baby, you can stay here as long as you please. When Devion gets in here from his shower, we are going to go over what I expect out of you two. Which brings me to the question, are you on birth control?"

I shake my head.

"Okay, well, I don't mean to get in your business, but you need to be. Not because you are with my son, but period, you don't need any slip-ups. Always remember, make sure you are good first before you let any man sneak a baby up in you."

Just from that, I know she has my best interest at heart, and it makes me want to shed a tear. Although all of this is new to me, I can tell Mama C is about business, and with her already telling me what is best for me, it feels genuine. I feel happiness bloom in my heart.

Chapter 10

The Awakening

Two months have passed since I moved in with Devion, and honestly, it has been nothing short of amazing. We have become more exclusive, and now, the whole school knows we a thing. Sometimes, it feels weird to have someone hold my hand and walk me to class, and to go home with the same guy. Of course, that still comes with eye-rolling and side-eye glances from these hating hoes at this school who thought they had a chance with him, but who cares? I do feel like I'm growing up too fast, though, like who do you know is a sophomore already staying with their boyfriend in high school? This some shit not everybody can relate to.

Also, I haven't seen or talked to Merceedes since I went by her house. I really think she is avoiding me. But with everything that has been going on, I haven't had time to worry about that girl. If she don't want to be friends after all of these years because I have a new man, so be it. That envy would have come out sooner or later. Now, Lynn and I have gotten extremely close, since I told her everything that has been going on, and she has been more supportive than expected. We are even at the point where I go to her house from time to time after school, and her household is better than I expected. Oddly, she hasn't talked to Merceedes either, so maybe I'm not the only problem.

On the living situation aspect, Mama C has definitely taken over the mature-mother role in my life. Since I have become sexually active, whether she likes it or not, she is not dumb. Within that following week of me moving in, she took me to Planned Parenthood to get on the pill, and I haven't been boosting and stealing for money because she even gives me money for helping her around the house. And I don't know what has been done or said to Lamont since that situation, but based off what I heard from Mama C's conversations with her other brothers and Devion, he has been missing ever since. His wife and two kids even came by the house, which was awkward as hell, but they haven't even seen him. Knowing that he has a daughter and a son, I wonder what he's put them through, or did he just do it to me? Mama C did once bring up if I wanted to press charges, but I'm not trying to relive all of that in the court. I will get my revenge eventually.

But I have something to confess. Things have been getting odd between me and Devion lately. I'm not sure if the honeymoon stage is deteriorating, but he has been pretty distant with me lately. We are still having sex periodically through the week, but even that isn't meaningful like the first time was. If anything, it is me half-asleep, turned to the side, while he gets his rocks off. I haven't enjoyed our sex in weeks. It feels more like a chore than anything, but it is definitely a disconnection. One day, I forgot to take my birth-control pill, and do you know, he flipped completely out and went on about how I am irresponsible and shit like that. I told him, "You can use a condom if it's such a problem."

Another thing, every time Devion's friend Marcus comes over, they have to be In the car or in another room talking. Marcus is weird to me, too. Every time he comes around, he is looking at me upside my head, and he doesn't even say hi. But back to Devion, he didn't start off like this at all. Now, when people call or FaceTime him, he walks out the room. Yesterday, we were laid up watching a BET movie—*Baby Boy*, to be exact. You know that damn movie comes on just about every other day. His phone was on the charger by my side of the bed. He received a text message, so I reached over to hand it to him, and of course I was going to glance and see who it was, but he snatched his phone out of my hands like I was annoying him or something. I couldn't believe he did that, and I sat there in utter shock.

Do he want me to leave or something? Is this how regular relationships go? I don't know, but I'm not going to sit here like a dumbass, I'm going to see wassup right when he gets home from hanging with friends after school.

Chapter 11

Friend of Mine

I finish my homework in enough time to clean Devion's room before he arrives home, and with Mama C gone to Bible study until seven, we have more than enough time to talk out our differences. Usually, when he wants to hang out with his friends, he gets home around four thirty. Lately, it has been a little later than that, but I don't think anything is going on to where we can't work it out. So, I hurry up and get in the shower and I put on a tight fitted romper that shows my curves, with his favorite Victoria's Secret perfume. Before I made it home, I managed to pick up some of his favorite snacks for when we make up, so we can bond and watch a new movie or something. So far, we usually bond by watching movies and talking, so why not recreate a setting that we are comfortable with?

While I am cleaning his room, I go as far as organizing his papers in his desk drawer. To my surprise, I find a notebook of letters that are composed for me. It looks like a bunch of rough drafts to me, because every page starts with, "Hey, Chanel, you know I love you, and I have something to tell you . . ." Another even says, "To my future wife . . ." What if he plans on proposing to me, and that's why he has been acting funny?! Yeah, I'm going to have to be extra romantic tonight. Maybe I need to hurry and go to the corner store before he gets home. Maybe one of them drunks that be in front of the corner store can go in and get a bottle for me.

While I'm setting up, I hear the screen door slam. He made it home earlier than I expected. So, I rush downstairs to greet him, smiling and holding his favorite snacks in my hand, contemplating whether I should ask him about the notebook. As I turn the corner into the living room, I notice it isn't just Devion in the house, he has a whole bitch with him. They're sitting on the couch.

"What the fuck? Merceedes? Ummm, what are you doing here? How did you even know where I am living?" I look around the room and give a death stare to Devion. He can't even look me in my eyes, which gives me an indication that something is up.

Merceedes gets up with her well-rounded stomach showing under her flowing sundress. "Are you going to tell her or not?"

I step back in surprise, my stomach beginning to knot up to the point where I don't know what's happening to me.

Devion proceeds to put his head in his hands as if he's defeated. I can't do anything but stand there. It feels like someone has put a knife through my back and hasn't taken it out yet.

"If he isn't going to tell you, well, I will. Clearly, he—WE are expecting a baby. I didn't feel the need to tell you because I didn't think y'all would even get this far, but I guess he likes to be captain save-a-hoe. I really felt bad for you, and with us not being together, I was trying to be nice and let you dream."

Devion tries to walk toward me and says, "Baby, I really didn't mean for this to happen. I didn't even know y'all were friends. Merceedes and I were never together, we were just fucking. I don't even know if it's mines!"

"Not yours? Bitch, you know damn well it is, and we still have been fucking, since you been staying with this nigga. He is right about one thing, he didn't know we knew each other, but one thing I am not is someone's secret. The same shit he has done for you, he will do for me even better. We were never friends, bitch, now go get raped by his Uncle Smoke."

As I soak all that has happened in, something in me breaks and I lunge at Merceedes. Devion pushes me back, but I run up again and spit dead-smack in the middle of her face. "I fucking trusted the both of you, how could y'all do this to me?! What exactly did I do to deserve this?" I scream as I look into Devion's pathetic hazel eyes.

I push Devion, fix my romper, and head up the stairs. I guess the fairy tale isn't meant for everyone. I don't know where I am going. I only have a hundred dollars to my name, but I have to get the hell out of here. It's fine, I will find a way like I always do. My hands and legs are shaking so hard, I can barely keep my composure as I rush to pack my things. While I am packing, I have flashes in my head of all of the signs that I have missed, and it all comes to me. It's been in my face! That's why the bitch has been acting funny! But I'm still confused—she hasn't liked me since the third grade? I have been through some shit, but this takes the cake.

All of these things are running through my mind a mile a minute. Did his mama know?! Do the people in our school know? How could I have been so blind to all of this?! If Devion really loved me, he wouldn't have let this happen and let me look so damn stupid after all of this time. You know what? It's fine, though. Going to church with Mama C has taught me God will always make a way. And he wouldn't put nothing on me that I can't handle. So, I guess I dodged a bullet . . . but if I had a gun, they would be dodging my bullets, too.

Chapter 12

Fool Me One Time, Shame on You

I download the Uber app and put in the cheapest motel I can find. I see Motel 6 is having a special for fifty-five dollars a night, and that should be able to tide me over for one night. After that, I am just going to take things day by day. All I know is I have to get the hell out of dodge. As I wait for my phone to notify me of the Uber's arrival, I make sure that I have all of my belongings in my duffel bag and suitcase. I even went through some of Devion's dresser drawers to see what money I could find. I managed to scrape up a hundred and twenty dollars, and that can be food money and some extra. He won't miss this little money; I will consider this a small payment on the debt he owes me for putting me through this.

Twenty minutes have passed, and I am just now notified that my Uber is here. I grab my shit, walk down the stairs, and before I reach the door, I glance over to see Merceedes's arm wrapped around Devion, comforting him while he is staring at the ground with tears falling down his nose. I throw the front door open and place my belongings in the backseat of the Uber and get in. I can't help but notice Devion's friend Marcus standing by the driver's door of Devion's car, trying his best to hold his laugh in as the Uber pulls away from the front of the house.

One thing is for certain about me, I will survive. That's all I know how to do. When this is all said and done, I will have the last word and laugh.

Credits

First and foremost I would like to thank everyone that had a hand in creating this book. All of your hard work is truly appreciated and I am honored to have encountered everyone's creative touch.

The characters in this book are fictional. Furthermore any resemblance to any actual people alive or dead is coincidental.

www.ingramcontent.com/pod-product-compliance
Lightning Source LLC
Chambersburg PA
CBHW051359150726
48000CB00003B/1259